IRAN

Leslie C. Kaplan

The Tony Stead
NONFICTION
INDEPENDENT
READING COLLECTION

Rosen Classroom Books & Materials™
New York

To Mark from the S.C.F.

Published in 2006 by The Rosen Publishing Group, Inc.
29 East 21st Street, New York, NY 10010

First Edition

Editor: Rachel O'Connor
Book Design: Haley Wilson
Layout Design: Nick Sciacca
Photo Researcher: Adriana Skura

Photo Credits: Cover © Werner Forman/Corbis; p. 4 (inset) © Lex Farnsworth/The Image Works; p. 6 © Adam Woolfitt/Corbis; p. 6 (inset) © Dean Conger/Corbis; p. 8 © British Library/AKG London; p. 10 © Bettmann/Corbis; p. 12 © Shepard Sherbell/Corbis SABA; p. 12 (inset) © Didier Ermakoff/The Image Works; p. 14 © Topham/The Image Works; p. 16 © AP/Wide World Photos; p. 18 © Lachenmaier/Bilderberg/Aurora Photos; p. 19 © The British Library/Topham-HIP/The Image Works; p. 20 © Earl & Nazima Kowall/Corbis; p. 22 © Eyewire.

Library of Congress Cataloging-in-Publication Data
Kaplan, Leslie C.
A primary source guide to Iran / Leslie C. Kaplan.— 1st ed.
    v. cm. — (Countries of the world, a primary source journey)
Includes bibliographical references and index.
Contents: A look at Iran—Land and weather—Iran's history—Trying for a new Iran—The government—The economy—A Muslim nation—The arts—Iran today—Iran at a glance.
ISBN 1-4042-5548-6
1. Iran—Juvenile literature. [1. Iran.] I. Title. II. Series.
DS254.75.K37 2005
955–dc22
                                        2003019933

Manufactured in the United States of America

Contents

KAZAKHSTAN

CASPIAN SEA

Sea of Azov

BLACK SEA

Bosporus

GEORGIA

ARMENIA
AZERBAIJAN

UZBEKISTAN

KYRGYZSTAN

TURKMENISTAN

TURKEY

KURDISTAN

TAJIKISTAN

CYPRUS
LEBANON

SYRIA

IRAQ

TEHRAN

IRAN

AFGHANISTAN

KASHMIR
(Disputed
Territory)

JORDAN

KUWAIT

Persian

Gulf

PAKISTAN

INDIA

RED SEA

QATAR

U.A.E.

Gulf of Oman

SAUDI ARABIA

OMAN

ARABIAN SEA

INDIAN

OCEAN

Iran, in southwestern Asia, is one of the biggest countries in the Middle East. Iran's location between Europe and Asia has made it a popular place for **explorers**, traders, and travelers for thousands of years. Iran is bordered by the Caspian Sea and the countries of Turkmenistan, Armenia, and Azerbaijan to the north. The Persian Gulf and the Gulf of Oman border Iran to the south. The countries of Pakistan and Afghanistan are east of Iran. Turkey and Iraq border Iran to the west.

◀ Iran lies where Europe and Asia meet. *Inset:* More than one-sixth of the population, about 12 million people, live in Iran's crowded capital city, Tehran.

Land and Weather

About two-thirds of Iran is either a desert or mountain area. The center of Iran is a large **plateau** with two large deserts. Mountains surround the plateau.

Iran's weather is very dry. The northern parts of Iran along the Caspian Sea have the country's best soil for farming. Many Iranians live in this area. In southern Iran, the winters are mild and the summers are very hot.

◀ Two Iranian women and their children walk past a field of young crops on the Caspian coast. *Inset:* An important river, the Shatt al Arab, runs between Iran and Iraq.

Throughout history, Iran's borders have gone through several changes. In the mid-500s B.C., under the rule of Persian King Cyrus II, Iran grew to include Egypt, parts of Asia, northern India, and parts of Greece. At other times, Iran was much smaller. The Arabs took over Iran in A.D. 651 when it was called Persia and ruled it until the 1000s. The Arabs introduced the **religion** of **Islam** to the people of Iran and taught them to speak Arabic.

◀ This painting shows an army from Mongolia taking over Iran. The Mongols ruled Iran from 1220 until the 1400s.

Iran's Leaders

Reza Khan became Iran's leader in 1925 and changed his name to Reza Pahlavi. He built Iran's first railroad, created its first university, and built highways, factories, and seaports. Under Pahlavi's rule, Islamic leaders lost some of their power and their land. His son, Mohammad Reza Pahlavi, became Iran's leader in 1941. In 1979, a **revolution** broke out and Pahlavi fled the country. Ruhollah Khomeini took over and changed Iran back to the **traditional** rules of the Islamic way of life.

◀ This photograph from 1925 shows Reza Pahlavi in his army uniform.

The Government

The book of Islam, known as the Qur'an or Koran, has laws about many parts of life. After the 1979 revolution, these laws were once again closely followed by government leaders. The highest-ranking religious leader, called a ***faqih***, has power over the government and Iran's armed forces. Religious leaders serve as judges. Iran has a president who is elected by the people every 4 years. Iran also has a **parliament** that is elected by the people to make Iran's laws.

◀ The Iranian parliament holds their meetings in this room.
Inset: Shown here is the Qur'an.

Although it is hard to grow crops in Iran because of the mountain areas and dry weather, more than one-quarter of Iranians work in farming. Iran is the world's largest producer of dates. Iran also has a lot of oil. Oil makes up four-fifths of Iran's **exports**. Many Iranians also work in businesses such as mining, car **manufacturing**, carpets, and cloth.

◄ Here an Iranian shepherd feeds his sheep.
Inset: The rial is the unit of money used in Iran.

15

Almost all of Iran's people are Muslims. A Muslim is someone who follows the religion of Islam. Muslims believe that there is only one god, Allah. They go to mosques (MAHSKS) to pray to Allah. The Islamic religion is controlled by men. Islamic law has rules about how men and women dress and act in public. Women can go to school, work, and vote, but are expected to obey men.

◀ Before entering a mosque, Muslims must remove their shoes and wash their hands, faces, and feet. In this photograph, Muslims gather at a mosque to pray.

この店の品物
直接取引です
従って仲介者
の手数料は取
せん自然の
テーブルクロス

18

Iran is famous for its handmade carpets. The carpets are found in most Iranian homes and are sold around the world. Iranian artists paint pictures in a

special style that uses very small figures. Poetry is the most well-known form of Iranian writing. The most famous poet in Iran was Omar Khayyám, who lived from about 1048 B.C. to about 1131 B.C.

Here a carpet seller is surrounded by beautiful handmade carpets at an Iranian market. *Above:* Omar Khayyám's most well-known book of poetry has about 600 poems.

19

Mealtime in Iran

Meals are an important part of family life in Iran. Rice is often mixed with meat such as lamb or chicken and vegetables. Flatbread or other kinds of wheat bread and sometimes different cheeses are often eaten with the main meal of the day. Popular drinks include sweetened tea and a drink made with yogurt. Fresh fruits are often eaten at the end of the meal.

◀ In Iran, families sit on the floor to share a meal.

Population: 69,018,924

Capital City: Tehran, population about 12,000,000

Official Name: Islamic Republic of Iran

National Anthem: "Soroude Jomhun-ye Eslami-ye Iran" ("Anthem of Islamic Republic of Iran")

Land Area: 636,300 sq miles (1,648,017 sq km)

Government: Republic, but with authority held by the highest-ranking religious leader under laws of Islam

Languages: Persian, Turkic, Kurdish, Luri, Balochi, Arabic, Turkish

Unit of Money: Rial

Flag: The flag has green, white, and red stripes. Green stands for Islam, white means peace, and red is for the bravery of the Iranian people.

Glossary

explorer (ik-SPLOR-uhr) A person who travels in search of adventure, land, or money.

export (EHK-sport) Goods sent to other countries for sale.

faqih (fah-KEE) A leader of the Islamic faith.

Islam (is-LAHM) A faith based on the teachings of Muhammad and the Qur'an.

manufacture (man-yuh-FAK-chur) To make goods by hand or by machine.

parliament (PAR-luh-munt) A group of people who make the laws for a country.

plateau (plah-TOH) A broad, flat area of high land.

religion (rih-LIH-juhn) Having to do with a faith; a system of beliefs.

revolution (reh-vuh-LOO-shun) A complete change in government.

traditional (truh-DIH-shuh-nuhl) Having to do with handing down of information, beliefs, or ways of a family or group.

Index

Primary Source List

Page 4 (inset). Overview of the city of Tehran. April 1998. Photograph by Lex Farnsworth.
Page 6. Two Iranian women and their children on the Caspian Coast, Iran. Circa 1970–1995. Photograph by Adam Woolfitt.
Page 6 (inset). Overview of the Shatt al Arab River. Abadan, Iran. 1968. Photograph by Dean Conger.
Page 8. Originally a part of the epic poem *Timurnameh* by Persian poet Abdullah Hatifi, this sixteenth-century painting depicts the capture of Isfahan by Timur and his Mongolian armies in 1388.
Page 10 Portrait of Reza Khan, Shah of Iran, dressed in his military uniform. November 1925.

Web Sites

Due to the changing nature of Internet links, the Rosen Publishing Company, Inc., has developed an online list of Web sites related to the subject of this book. This site is updated regularly. Please use this link to access the list: **http://www.powerkidslinks.com/cwpsj/psiran/**